P9-DUT-101

↥

THE MIRACLE HATER

A Novel by

Shulamith Hareven

Translated from the Hebrew
by Hillel Halkin

NORTH POINT PRESS
San Francisco 1988

Copyright © 1988 by Shulamith Hareven
English translation copyright © 1988 by Hillel Halkin
Printed in the United States of America
Library of Congress Catalogue Card Number: 87-82580
ISBN: 0-86547-329-3

North Point Press
850 Talbot Avenue
Berkeley, California
94706

▶ THE MIRACLE HATER ◀

They kept leaving all the time. One from a town, two from a family, they fled the settled districts of the land of Egypt to join those who had left before them. They did not go far: no further than the nearest oasis or the first gully that had a spring. They sought only to put the sand between themselves and Egypt, to get away from its lords and officials. No more than that.

They had no leaders. Perhaps no customs either. They dwelt in their oases, where they led lives of lowly, grinding, sunbaked poverty, shuffling about in black rags, whistling to their flocks that were as black and gaunt as they, often subsisting on robbery. Now and then troops were sent out to restore order; yet this did not happen often, for such expeditions were known to be perilous. The barefoot oasesdwellers could deal the soldiers a quick, sharp blow and melt off into the sands where even the wind lost all track of them. Year after year the corpses left by both sides were scorched by the sun until they could no longer be told apart from the bones of the earth itself. Every bit of yarn or iron had been stripped from them long ago.

Occasionally, half stealth and half insolence, known by his black rags, by the deep, grimy bronze of his tough, saurian hide, and by the furtive way he moved, one of the fugitives would approach the adobe wall of a farm. His shadow flitted over it like a raven's; whoever sensed it, remarked: There goes one of them. Then, a teal snatched from a canal or a watermelon in season wrapped in the folds of his cloak, he bounded quickly back into the desert, leaving behind him a mocking flurry of oaths. The farm workers drove him off lackadaisically, staring at his brazen flight with a stolid, passive amazement.

People held them in low repute. Vagabonds, they were

called contemptuously, castaways. Not even the poorest slave, not even the meanest day laborer, would give his daughter in marriage to anyone belonging to this outcast band of Hebrews. In fact, though, little was seen of them. Those who left had left for good. The sand ruled them off utterly from the denizens of the watered farmland with its canals and ditches, its seasons and crop cycles, its masters and slaves, its borders and hedges, its settled ways that revolved as slowly each day as the water buffalo turns around the waterwheel.

Sanded in, bound to no man, they waited.

There were others too. Long settled in one place, they had become like Egyptians. At any time one of their boys might be spied perched high in a date grove on a ladder propped against a palm frond, harvesting the clusters of fruit with a short knife, or covering their heavy, pendulous abundance with a net against the multitude of birds, or simply staring down at the crossroads below while playing away on a flute. They belonged to the house of Tsuri, mastersingers and musicians without peer who worked for the wealthy families of Raamses and lived in spacious homes in the shade of the date palms. Walking out toward evening to the nearby canal, they stood bathed in a great, golden radiance, in the honeyed, leonine light pouring over the plain, fishing with the Egyptian boys, sometimes with hooks and nets from the bank and sometimes from their high-sparred boats. Barefoot and wet, dripping light and sparkles of water, they brought their catch home in panniers full of quivering, silvery, sinewy fish, their voices mingling with the calls of the gorgeous birds that fished at this hour too. Wherever man made way, hordes of pelicans, pink flamingoes, white egrets, and ibises descended with a great flap of wings and no end of commotion.

This hour of Egypt's grace was never missed by the lady Ashlil, a Hebrew woman who was the widow of a local official. Stepping out on her rooftop thatched with palm fronds, she peeled the fruit handed her by one of her young male attendants and leisurely watched the light slowly dropping like dark honey over the ambering, the silvering, the darkling water. Many years before, while still an unbetrothed girl, she had seen, at precisely this time of day, a leopard with man's eyes standing by the old canal that had since fallen into disuse. Now, every evening, her keen eyes were trained on that spot. But there were no leopards, only the white egrets that followed the water buffaloes, and the Hebrew hands shouldering their burdens and singing their hushed songs in which there was not a shred of hope. The Hebrews had multiplied greatly and not all of them could find work in and around Raamses. They descended on the province, innumerable flocks of men and women who stood long hours in the sun, or sat in the shade of the baked-brick walls, looking for work. The Egyptians would come, take the five or ten of them that they needed, and drive the rest off. For a while they would vanish; yet soon they were back again, mute in the fly-ridden sunlight, waiting. Even when the busy season was over in the fields they went on waiting, more of them every year. There was no getting rid of them. In the end they were forbidden to bear children. It was time they squatted elsewhere. It was time they went away. But the Hebrews did not go. Their wives cunningly gave birth in secret lairs and were back at work a few hours later. Often they could not retrieve the newborn child from its hiding place. Wild animals sniffed out the lairs.

On the feast of Osiris, when, in an ark made of bulrushes, each Egyptian household floated a painted, decorated little image of the god upon the Nile and its great canals, the wives of the Hebrew laborers cunningly floated their infants on the water too. Sometimes these arks came to rest in the tall, silent reeds; sometimes the foundlings were rescued by Egyptian families, who took them to be the annual reincarnation of the god Osiris himself. This was nothing to wonder at: everybody knew that life and death belonged to the Nile, that most supreme, that mightiest of rivers whose vast waters were the water of life. Even barren women whose wombs had turned to wood and stone were known to have conceived through them. Sometimes it was enough to suck on the rushes in the thick growth by the riverside in order to become pregnant. Where, if not from the same slime, did all those millions of frogs, all that ceaseless fecundity, come from?

Baita was nearly five years old when the hired hand Milka gave birth to Eshkhar, in total darkness, in a hidden burrow at the far end of the Hebrews' camp. She had stumbled down there during the day and now stood frightened in one corner, a thumb in her mouth, listening to the unseen squatting woman laboring to deliver her child. At first Baita thought that she had descended to this place in order to empty her bowels. The burrow was hot, cramped, and full of grunts, like the presence of a host of furry beasts. Milka paid no attention to Baita, who, watching from where she crouched in the corner, strove to make out the dim shapes, to decipher the darkness and the heat.

Then, as if the furry animals had gone, it was over. The burrow became empty and clean. A gust of wind, a thirsty night breeze, blew down into it; the clouds broke away from the moon and a whitish light shone inside. Milka rose groaning. She wiped herself and her baby and carried it to the entrance of the burrow. A boy, she grunted to herself. A boy.

She tied his cord with a piece of string and, taking a date from her clothing, chewed it carefully and smeared its pulp with her thumb on his palate. He whimpered a bit and fell still.

Then she saw Baita, eyes gleaming in the corner. Wearily she asked if she had been there all the time. Baita nodded.

For a long while Milka said nothing. Then, digging a hole with a peg she had brought, she thoughtfully buried the afterbirth and the other remains. Finally, with a quick motion, she placed the naked, shivering child in Baita's arms.

9

—Take him home with you. His name is Eshkhar.

Baita clutched the boy and ran with him to her father's hut. Though the women there sought to take him from her, she refused to part with him. It was all they could do to persuade her to let them change her soaked clothes. The child was as much her own as if she had borne him herself. She laid him down close to her and did not fall asleep until morning came with the scrabble of chickens among the thatched shacks, the creaky rounds of the buffalo tied to its wheel, the thump-and-stomp of the cattle being taken out to pasture, the splash of fresh milk into jugs, all the clamor and commotion of watering troughs. Eshkhar slept at her side.

Sometimes it was Milka who nursed him, always hurriedly between chores; sometimes one of the women from the house of her father Yitzhar, anyone who happened to have milk in her breasts. Sometimes Baita herself dripped fatty yellow buffalo milk into his mouth. He'll be sick, they warned her. But Eshkhar grew up and thrived. Eventually they strapped him to her back, so that, when dusk dropped, one might have thought that a strange, humped little animal was roaming the village and bleating from its hump.

One tuft of Baita's hair was always wet from being sucked by the child. Always the same one.

They grew up as one body.

A year or so later, Milka, who now went to work each day in an Egyptian house, was large with child again. She had been admonished not to take chances, but, apart from binding her stomach to keep it well in, made light of the advice. There's no harm in them, she said. The Egyptian maids were all her friends, and besides, if she did not go to work, who would feed all those hungry children whose father could be counted on for nothing? Yet her time came sooner than she had calculated and found her shaking out her mistress's rugs. She sought to slip off to the fields, but was seen by a little servant who ran to tell the lady of the house. The lady was in mourning that week for a son who had died, and could not bear the thought of a Hebrew giving birth when she herself was bereaved. What can explain this dreadful fertility of the Hebrews, she was wont to lament to her husband, except their working in the mud of the Nile, which everyone knows is good for childbearing? Just look how they've settled down to spawn here with the frogs, flies, and lice; will you tell me when we ever had so many frogs and flies before? We go around scratching as though with the mange because of their filth. They've taken all the blessing from our lives. This plaint was spoken in a hoarse, throaty timbre and accompanied by the melancholy, slow, unceasing tinkle of her anklets. Now, when her little maidservant came to tell her that the Hebrew woman was in labor, she jumped to her feet and an evil thought came out of her like a spark. She summoned the Canaanite overseer, an evil-hearted man. A great hush settled over the house and all its frightened occupants. The Canaanite seized Milka, tied her by the feet, and hung her head-down from the nearest tree. All day long her swollen belly heaved horribly like a dying fish, making the tree, the village, the earth itself shudder. Then it stopped.

When night came, several of the Hebrew men set out. They knew they would not catch the Canaanite. But they did waylay a wagon of Egyptians. It was the feast of the firstborn, and the Egyptians were off to celebrate in a painted cart decorated with bulrushes and feathers. Most of them were tipsy. They never heard the lurking fury ahead. They had no foreboding of it. The Hebrews murdered them quickly, every one of them, eldest sons all, from the age of five to twenty. In silence they worked, panting with fear, in a cold sweat; then fled. Hurry, hurry, they urged their wives, we cannot even stay until the morning. They took what they could and quickly made for the sands.

Afterwards they waited for the punitive expedition. It never came. Still, the fear remained and they kept moving further away, until even the pointed tips of Egypt's scattered pyramids could no longer be seen on the horizon. There was nothing but sand. On the fifth day they found the camp of the castaways, those who had left the settled land long before them and pitched their tents nearby. At first they spoke to them haughtily: *they* would yet return to Egypt, they were just waiting for things to blow over, for the old pharaoh to die. But the castaways laughed in their faces. You can never go back, they said, never. You might as well get used to it now.

They waited. Gradually they too built booths and mud huts in their new abode. And went on waiting.

Once Moses came. He arrived secretly, accompanied by only one man, who kept his silence. A boy waited atop a small dune for them to appear and led them wordlessly to the camp.

13

They were more surprised than impressed by Moses' appearance. It was said that he had killed an Egyptian; that he had fled for his life far across the desert, all the way to the distant Ancestral Land; and that, unapprehended, he had returned from there. Some said that he had two hearts in his breast, one Hebrew and one Egyptian, and that he had murdered the Egyptian one so as to leave no trace of it. Some even swore that they had seen the scar on his chest. Yet although he did not quite seem a Hebrew like the rest of them, there was nothing obviously Egyptian about him either. Egypt was all eloquence and ceremony, whereas he had trouble talking and spoke the Hebrew language quite clumsily. The more slowly he talked, though, the more quickly he paced back and forth while gesturing with his hands, his prognathous beard pointing forward as though he knew his exact destination. He was tall and broad-shouldered, yet seemed ashamed of it, as if he did not want to be a cut above anyone, so that he hunched himself down with a winning, likeable modesty. Sometimes an Egyptian word slipped into his speech, causing him to blush all over. He told them that it was time to go.

There were among them, they said to him, some who

talked a great deal about returning to the Ancestral Land. Yes, yes, he answered distractedly, as if the point lay elsewhere. The point was to go. All of them. Even those who were still in Egypt. To become one clan, together. Together. He joined his two large hands, as if to show them how closely, how inextricably together he meant.

His Egyptian childhood oppressed him; he was unable to free himself of it. He talked to them about eternity, that of life and that of death, and was forced to resort to Egyptian. He spoke of the mummies by which the Egyptians made death last forever, and of a burning red berry bush in the desert that was deathless life. Although they did not understand him, they nodded politely, without arguing. If the man wanted to talk about burning bushes, let it be burning bushes. Then he asked how many of them could live as shepherds. This was an easier question, one they could readily answer: most of them, they told him, in fact nearly all of them, even those who more recently had worked as builders, or as farmhands, or in the waterworks. The Hebrews are a people of shepherds, they said. They eat the sheep, and wear the sheep, and sleep with the sheep to keep warm. At that his face lit up, as if a more pleasurable reply could not have been imagined; he clapped hand against hand, shining all over, until they were amazed.

After this he took his leave of them and returned with his escort, who still had not spoken a word. The same boy who had brought them led them back to where they could see the long green line that was Egypt. There he halted, spat, and retraced his steps again.

They kept on leaving, and those who had left now formed a large camp. Not all of them lived together. The desert was huge, though scattered about in it were lonely Egyptian farms with cattle pens hedged in by low brick walls and little fields of beans and clover—more gardens really than fields—whose green was flecked with white egrets. The Hebrews kept away from these farms. Here and there half-savage armed guards watched them as they passed, matching stare for stare until they were gone.

One could no longer easily say how many of them there were. The camp swelled with each passing month and year, and a day's walk in any direction brought one to more camps. By day and by night wondrous stories made the rounds. It was said that Moses had had a great fight with Pharaoh himself. That he had vanquished all the sorcerers of Egypt. That his staff had turned into a leopard, a lion, a deer. That he had brought death upon all the firstborn of Egypt. That he had brought plague and pestilence. They themselves were not sure if they believed these stories or not. They told them hesitantly, with a slightly vacant expression that was followed by a short, nervous laugh. They waited. By now there was no returning to the heart of Egypt, yet they knew that they could not long remain where they were. Meanwhile the strange stories filled their days. Baita too, who sat in a corner with Eshkhar in her lap, listened to them avidly. It was rather odd for some of them to hear such tales about Moses, whose mother Yokheved, a woman gone dotty with age, they knew well. Still, no one denied them.

And then they were told that they were setting out.

The grace-light of a broad sunset flooded the land. Flocks of egrets wheeled overhead as if searching for the light's end. Nimbly in the camp below the boys seized the bleating sheep. From out of the houses came voices, bellows, shouts, and croaks. Straw baskets and panniers stood outside, packed and tied with hemp that had run out, so that, by each doorway, people crouched by twos and threes weaving more as quickly as they could. Bundle was piled upon bundle. Women wrapped fruit in broad leaves and tied clusters of dates to long poles. Here and there things broke in the rush. A smell of roast meat, of blood, of spilled beverage, and of date honey hung in the swiftly darkening air. The trampled, muddy clay paths of the camp glittered in the sunset, and later in the flickering light of the torches, with a gross, dark, bloody sheen. It was almost as if the quick of life itself, now shamelessly exposed for all to see, were being readied for transfer to some other place: the utensils of women thrown about out-of-doors, the now useless guts of sheep, the chamber pots and slop bowls, broken shards, the bare frame of a spinning wheel that never would spin again.

With the first stars the bonfires leaped higher. The time for the paschal sacrifice had come. Hurry, urged the elders, hurry. Swiftly, with light strokes, the knife was wielded and cuts of meat were thrown into the flames by the boys. They ate in haste, standing in front of their houses or at the ends of the muggy lanes, ripping the meat apart with their fingers, which dripped half-raw fat, and smearing it on the walls and the doorposts. Some of the women served large leaves of lettuce and celery to wipe up with. Hurry, urged the elders, hurry. The boys leaped forward to stamp out the fires and scatter the coals. Some made water on the embers. More torches were lit and the camp seethed.

They shouldered their possessions and set out, suddenly silent, strung out in a long line, the children clinging to the edges of their parents' robes. The lady Ashlil, who had arrived in camp unbeknownst, walked erect among them, her large bundles borne by her manservants. The house of Yitzhar shuffled along in its usual disarray, as if it had forgotten or left something behind. Baita walked in its midst, her hand held by Eshkhar, who, barefoot, looked curiously about him, sucking a sugarcane. In the unsteady light the herds and flocks separated each group and household from the others. There were not many torches. A great blackness loomed before and behind them.

The throng kept swelling. Everywhere more people fell in line. Near one of the camps the column was joined by the house of Tsuri, bearing their musical instruments, though they marched now in silence without playing. In bare feet, in sandaled feet, they walked on, over low hummocks and hillocks and dunes, to the clink of their earth-

enware vessels and the snorts and grunts of their animals.
On and on. In the gateways of the scattered farms along the
way stood an occasional Egyptian who watched the noc-
turnal procession go by in astonishment, as silent as the
marchers.

By the time dawn broke on the abandoned Hebrew
camp thousands of people had passed into the sands and
vanished there. A breeze rippled through the thatch of the
deserted huts. Here and there along the road leading to the
great desert lay bits of broken pottery, strewn fascicles of
beans, the sole of a disintegrated shoe.

Clouds of birds and flies swarmed down on the empty
camp.

An immense freedom, vast beyond human measure, hung over everything. The days had no rules and the laws of nature themselves seemed suspended. There was no longer any need to rise for work in the morning. There were no masters and no slaves. There was only the desert, which held no threat, and the gullies among the rocks. And the fresh, boundless mornings with the thinnest of mists rising from the thorn trees and from the flowering star thistles in the plain. The silence was palpable. There was no end of sky.

People had lived before them in the plain. Skulls and

parts of skeletons, not all of them human, were found in
the gullies. Eshkhar hated and feared these bones. Those
are day-yed Egyptians, he would say, clinging to Baita, always giving the word two syllables. Baita told him that a
dead Egyptian turned into a crocodile or a jackal. His *ba*
and *ka* came to take his soul and put it in another creature.
But a Hebrew didn't turn into anything. He was just buried. In the end some boys took a few sacks, collected these
relics, and dumped them far away. One of the younger boys
kept a giant jawbone, bigger than any ever seen.

Sometimes, before the break of dawn, someone would
awake in a fit of wild joy and roust out all his neighbors.
Then the sun would come up on an unwashed, unruly,
shimmying camp dancing in great festive circles. They
called these days holy days. But they had no need for words.
Occasionally, in the middle of the night, as though in a
drunken stupor, men would barge into Moses' tent and
wake him from his sleep. He should not put on airs. He
should not think that this was Egypt. He should not think
that he was pharaoh. Sometimes, when he passed through
the camp, he was accosted and slapped good-naturedly on
the back until his bones nearly broke: we're proud of you,

son of Amram, we just want you to know, you may be a
stammerer, they may have fished you from the Nile, but
we're proud of you all the same, even if we know all about
your mother Yokheved and those heathenish teraphim she
sits on in her tent like a mother hen on its eggs, you're our
boy and we love you, you thicktongue. And Moses, who
could not stand being touched, would control himself with
a precarious smile, his stammer getting worse, and make
his way through the good-humored stench. In those days
he considered it important to be seen by everyone. Yet he
seldom got as far as the tent of Yitzhar at the hindmost end
of the camp. Its dwellers were by no means the most distinguished of the families of Israel.

One day Nun came to Moses. He spoke Egyptian and
importuned him greatly, thrusting an obsequious hand
into his belt to make him yield. He had brought his son
Joshua with him; let Moses take him as his aide and body-
guard to protect him from the crowds that were so lovingly,
glad-handedly free with him that soon they would kill him
with affection. Moses would rather have declined, but
ended up by agreeing. From then on anyone wishing to see
him had first to get past Joshua, who sat by the flap of his

tent. There was some grumbling, but he was no longer harassed as before.

There were no sounds. A few bleats or whinnies from the flocks, a few human voices from the gully or the spring, now and then the sharp screech of some bird. All the sounds of settled land had been washed from their ears. The shouts of their taskmasters too.

Baita, make a sound like a water buffalo, Eshkhar would plead. Make a sound like a turtledove. Make sounds like Egypt.

And she would make all those sounds to keep him from forgetting, perhaps to keep herself from forgetting too. They would suddenly come to her, such as a certain stridulation of noontime which, when heard from afar, could be either a roosting rock pigeon, a chirping cricket, or the waterwheel creaking slowly around. A sound of the fields. In low tones she clucked it to him, enchanting both him and herself, her eyes shut as if actually seeing before her the broad green fields of clover and beans that stretched to the far horizon of Egypt.

Every night some fled the camp. They hungered for the greens and the fish, for the mighty murmur of living water

flowing serenely down the Nile, perhaps too for the sight
of a thin, high-sparred boat skimming soundlessly across a
low moon. Without a word they stole back to Egypt. Once
a party of five men was sent to the sea for salt. None of them
reached it. They returned to Egypt instead, where they as-
saulted some fishermen and ate the whole catch that was
lying in their holds. They wolfed it down raw, bones, guts,
and all, fish, mussels, and clams. Afterwards they grew bold
and took to thieving in the nearby towns. Within days they
quarreled over the gold, and in the end only one of them
came back, bringing no salt. It did him no good to protest
his innocence. One of the elders raised an angry hand at
him and killed him. No more salt parties were sent out.

At night there was fear. No one talked about it. The immense emptiness drove them close to each other, where
they lay huddled under a weave of palm shoots. At times
they still dreamed that Pharaoh's army had come to look
for them in the desert; at times of the green banks and the
mud of the Nile, or of Egypt's huge ashlars and statues.
Fear alone kept even more of them from returning. In their
sleep the entire desert rose to crush them with the most dismal of possible deaths. They trembled with terror and with

cold. Each morning the sun was a miracle of redemption. Somehow they never quite believed that it would come again to rescue them from the night.

Baita would tell Eshkhar stories to keep him from running away or from going off to play with the older boys. Yet he could not be tethered anymore. He disappeared for whole days at a time, with Aviel, with Zemer, with Joshua's brother Yakhin, to appear again in the evening like a penitent little animal and lay his head in her lap. Then, as if their bodies were wiser than they and wiser than all words and deeds, their lost peace returned. Once he told her that he no longer believed that there was such a place as Egypt. There was no Ancestral Land either. It was all fairy tales.

Year by year they grew poorer. The clothing taken with them from Egypt was wearing out. They moved from place to place in the desert, hopping back and forth among its few springs, from tamarisk to zizyph tree, their comings and goings pointless apart from the needs of their flocks. The terrain was rather hilly and very dry, yet they grew used to it. They learned to find and gather the juniper manna and to keep themselves and their animals away from the poisonously narcotic henbane. The pits from their dates and the dried dung from their flocks were saved to be added to the fires. Here and there they managed to sow, reap, and grind a bit of grain, enough for a bushel or two. Far ahead of them, in front of the camp, a huge bonfire, whose pillars of smoke and of fire were seen clearly by day and by night, was kept burning. No one strayed very far; if one of the shepherds wandered off until the low hills hid the fire from sight, he quickly headed back in a panic as if he had stumbled on some godless place and were now seeking absolution. There was no purpose to their lives. It simply was not Egypt. They had exchanged hard labor for freedom. Slavery was over but nothing else had taken its place. Old folk died and children grew up.

A time came when Yitzhar was seen thinking hard. Then he went to the Ephraimite tents and brought back an Ephraimite with him. They made a few calculations and, in the end, announced to the women that the maiden Baita would be given in marriage to a young Ephraimite named Zavdi, and that the bride-price was good.

Eshkhar stood by the entrance to the elders' tent. He was a skinny and not very tall boy about twelve years old. For a long while he waited restlessly, not daring to enter, until someone noticed him and motioned him inside.

He was unprepared for the darkness that reigned there. It was foreign and constricting, a far cry from the vast stretches of sand, the slanting light, and the low thickets of thorn trees; for whereas the household tents were always kept open, this one was shut and turned inward on itself. Tattered rugs covered the ground. Motes of dust swirled in the sunbeams that, like combs of light, fanned stripe by stripe through the joins of the tent cloths. Through the play of dust Eshkhar dimly discerned the faces of several of the elders. Yet they did not look the same as they did out-of-doors, so that he felt as if he did not know them. Standing with his back to him in a corner, pouring buttermilk into bowls, was the man who had signaled him to enter.

Someone asked him for his name and he answered, though so invisible was his questioner that he might as well have been talking to a shade. The man with the refreshment passed through the comb of light, glowing striped for a moment before fading out again, and served the bowls to the elders sitting opposite. Then there was silence once more, followed by a sound of slurping and whispers that Eshkhar could not make out. He stood waiting patiently. The dust danced before his eyes.

Finally he was asked what he wanted.

Something was puzzling him, he replied, something he did not understand. He knew, of course, that there was nothing to the beliefs of the Egyptians, and that the Hebrews did not think that there were any *bas* or *kas* who came to take your soul when you died. Yet the question bothered him whether or not one was born again after death, and if so, whether one's next life would be different from this one, or the same.

They were taken aback. Even in the dark he could sense their surprise. Suddenly he felt uncomfortable. He had thought that, being wise men and used to such questions, they must answer them all the time. Now he saw that he was wrong.

Wonderingly they asked him if he had not come to them for judgment: had someone robbed him of a lamb, or had some bread or garment been taken from his tent, or had the man whose flocks he tended done him wrong? Embarrassedly he answered no. Uneasy whispers were exchanged and a new voice inquired why he was asking such a thing. Was it just some riddle he had thought up? No, he said, no; it was more than that. See, his girl, Baita, the daughter of Yitzhar, had been betrothed to another man, and he wanted to know if this life was the only one they would have or if he could look forward to another in which amends would be made and he, Eshkhar, could take her, Baita, for his wife.

He was unprepared for the great peal of laughter that

31

erupted. It started with one of them and spread to the others. Gasping until they were hoarse they bawled into their buttermilk, their beards wagging, the tears streaming from their tired eyes. A lot they had seen and heard in this tent, but never the likes of this. And from whom? Why, from a young pup whose maleness was not yet even half-cocked. Someone has taken his pussy away and he wants to summon God to justice.

Eshkhar spun around and darted from the tent. Crying with anger and humiliation he bounded through the camp, running on and on until he came to where Moses dwelt. He would see Moses. He would tell him about the evil elders. Moses would judge him himself.

Joshua was sitting by the flap of the big tent, his curled side-whiskers gracing his broad moonface like two sentries standing guard. Spotlessly groomed, dressed all in white, he looked with disdain at the thin, grimy boy whose face was smeared with dirt and tears. What brings you to us, he asked with a barely perceptible stress of the last word. Eshkhar replied that he wished to see Moses. Joshua regarded him with a show of patience that was in fact anything but. We are resting now, he said. When we rest there is positively no entry. And after that we have business. Perhaps tomorrow. Perhaps the day after. If the boy would care to tell Joshua his problem, he, Joshua, of little account though he was, might be able to help.

Eshkhar let loose a tirade of words. They poured forth from him in an inarticulate babble, of which all Joshua heard was Yitzhar, Baita, elders, Yitzhar, bride-price, justice, justice, justice. The thinnest of smiles flitted over Joshua's chill lips without passing from them to the eyes, and he said:

—We work miracles. Justice is not our concern.

Whereupon he rose to his feet, his large white moonface filling the boy's field of vision. For an instant Eshkhar longed to poke his fist into its insolence and did not dare; yet Joshua, it seemed, read his thoughts well. Puffing his lips in triumph, he said:

—Go see the elders, boy, they'll justice-justice you all day long. Why, they pull each other's beards out, looking for justice there too. They make you come and go a hundredfold and still they don't find it for you. If the boy knew what was good for him he would take himself elsewhere, because already a gang of loiterers, damn them, was gath-

33

ering by the tent. Clear out of here right now or we'll be woken from our sleep. Get along with you now, scat!

At the entrance to Yitzhar's tent Eshkhar paused by the hanging gourd to wash his face and gulp great draughts of water. There was no one to help him but himself. And he would have to take Baita by himself, as a man took a woman; then she would be his and could never marry Zavdi anymore.

She was sitting in the tent, languidly waiting for the women to come and prepare her for the wedding ceremony. Anointed from head to toe with an unguinous, aromatic oil, her pomaded hair suffused with a sharp scent, she sat vacantly on a pile of sacks, her embroidered gown and jewelry in a corner, chafing her oiled arms as if to dry them; hearing Eshkhar's steps outside, however, she rose at once. What is it, her frightened eyes asked. But he did not answer. He fell upon her with all his might, embracing her, forcing her to the floor, striving to intertwine their legs; while she, stirred, let herself imagine for a moment that it was all a mistake, that rather than be brought to the house of Zavdi she was about to belong to her Eshkhar, who had grown overnight, as she was always meant to be; even now

34

she was yielding to him with a dreadful sweetness, even now her scented arms were around him and her mouth was open beneath his, clenched and unripe though it was.

But Eshkhar was still a boy. A moment later he pushed her away with a whimper and ran from the tent, ran far beyond the limits of the camp, where he threw himself down in the sand and sobbed as he rolled in it, rubbing against it as hard as he could to expunge what was left of the alien scent, of the last traces of his defeat.

He fled so far that he did not see Baita being brought to Zavdi's tent while the women sang and drummed all around her. Her eyes dilated, slightly drugged by all her unguents, she walked in their midst, hungry from fasting all day and embarrassed by all the commotion. Zavdi was a young man of almost eighteen with a still-unformed face, yet his hands were large and wise. All night long he gathered her to the piping of the flutes outside, the flutes of the house of Tsuri, and to the drumming of the women. Between one song and the next Baita's mother and aunts burst into the tent to seize the embroidered cloth and display her virginity to the guests. Then the merriment waxed even greater and the young men shouted cries of encouragement to Zavdi inside the tent: keep it up, Zavdi, they called, keep it up, you have the whole desert to water, or shall we come in there to help you? while Zavdi laughed heartily in the darkness: perdition take them, from highland to bushy lowland, he would water by himself.

Perfumed, ornamented, aroused, her hungry young body aching, Baita accepted him without question. Somehow it seemed to her that all the celebrating was just for a day or two, after which everything would be the same as before. In the morning, she thought, she would go see what had happened to Eshkhar. But morning found her weary of limb, her hair disheveled like a garden after a storm, with Zavdi deep in satisfied sleep by her side. She played with the scent locket around her neck and went nowhere.

Eshkhar fled to the remotest flocks, grinding his hatred between his teeth. His face was ashen and his movements slow and dreamlike, like a man under water. One day he returned to Yitzhar's tent. He did not so much as glance at the Ephraimite encampment, as if the very direction it lay in had ceased to exist. He wished, he said to Yitzhar, to start his own flock. Yitzhar hemmed and hawed a bit, but he knew the boy was right. Some day he would have to wive, beget, and set up house for himself, without a legal inheritance. Though he strove to drive a hard bargain, so did Eshkhar. He knew now that justice was on the side of the strong. Slowly he built up a flock. Quickly he learned to defend it. Once or twice a ewe with young was taken from him by force. He received blows and returned them. He made himself a big club and pastured far away. And when his friend Aviel came looking for him in the hills, he hid and did not show his face.

Then came the incident of the Dedanites.

Ever, ever so slowly, so slowly, in the saddles of their gigantic camels, in high, vertical waves, ballooning with each step to the chime of the coins and the tinsel that bordered their harnesses, the Dedanites came riding into the rear of the camp. Even their camels exuded arrogance. The Hebrews stood looking at them from the openings of their meager, scattered tents. They had many saddlebags.

The Dedanites wore funny hats with long neckcloths to protect them from the sun. Their beards were rather sparse.

They were heavily armed. The slaves who had followed them on foot leaped quickly forward to seize the bridles and bring the camels to their knees. Cumbersomely the Dedanites slipped to the ground, where they stood amid the loud grunts and belches of their mounts, some ten of them in all, surveying the crowd that had formed in the dismal camp. One of them said something in Canaanite that was not understood. Several of the Hebrews approached. The spokesman waited a moment, then switched to Egyptian. Seasoned travelers that they were, the Dedanites' first request was to be allowed to pay homage to their distinguished hosts' god, if only they might be shown his sanctuary.

The Hebrews had never been so dumbfounded in their lives. So complete was their bewilderment that they simply reddened and said nothing. The Dedanites waited politely. When no answer was forthcoming they reiterated their great desire to honor the god of their hosts, of whose great powers they had heard in the lands where they traded. Should it be his gracious pleasure they might perhaps sacrifice a slave or two to him, or else make him some other gift, all according to their hosts' custom. At last one of the elders morosely informed them that the god of his tribe was secret and did not show himself. The Dedanites barely managed to conceal their derisive smiles beneath their mustaches. A strange god indeed these people must have, said their faces. Perhaps he had gone to answer nature's call. Perhaps the god of the Hebrews was little and, when sought out, scuffled off to hide in the rocks like the coneys of the desert. But they proceeded with their business.

Verily they had heard that their hosts, the children of Israel, freemen and freemen's sons, had with them the riches of the land of Egypt, which their great and world-renowned god had graciously bestowed on them. If they would be good enough to grant a few days' hospitality, they, the Dedanites, would open all their saddlebags before them, every last one of them. Heaven forbid that they should hold back a thing, no, no, no; they had with them fine weaves, and embroidery, and the fruit of the almond tree, and handsome cookware, and gleaming flint vessels. Perhaps some of these worthless objects might find favor in their hosts' eyes. They would open everything, without exception; for they knew that the children of Israel were not desert brigands, perish the thought, and that not one thread of what they had brought to this distinguished place would be unaccounted for. Indeed, as for brigands, they had already dispatched fierce and powerful ones, whose bones now lay bleaching in the sands. Casually they touched the handles of their daggers as they spoke, an icy glitter in their eyes.

Someone signaled assent. In a trice the camp was transformed. The Dedanites' servants knelt and unpacked large, comfortable tents whose flaps were left opened wide. More and more onlookers arrived, forming a tight ring around them, curious to see how they sat and how they ate. The Dedanites, however, took their time. Only toward evening did one of them clap his hands, causing the saddlebags to be opened and their wares to be spread out upon rugs. The Hebrews stared in fascination all evening without buying a thing. Not until the next morning did one or two women shamefacedly step forward and emerge from a tent with a small vial of kohl. The human ring remained nearly intact.

For four whole days the Dedanites engaged in the minutest barter, a yard of cloth for some quail eggs dried in sand, a vial of balsam of hyssop for some date honey, cheaper than any that could be bought in Egypt. The trade they had come for, though, failed to materialize. They were certain that the treasures of Egypt were well hidden in the tents of these Hebrews. They refused to disbelieve in them. If the Hebrews had not plundered the wealth of the land of Egypt, they insisted in language that grew less and less ornate, why had they fled from there? Or could it be that the gold of Egypt had a call from nature too and was hiding in the desert like their little god, whom they clearly were ashamed of, since they would not show an idol or an image of him? They had been dealing in women's trifles, grumbled the Dedanites, in petty haggling that was not at all what they were here for. Come, come: where were all the brave men? Where were the true treasures on account of which they had fled Egypt, notorious bandits that they were, and eluded their pursuers to this day?

The Hebrews looked abashedly at each other and did not know what to say. Never before had it struck them how poor they really were. So poor that even the flies that had followed them from Egypt and were once always in the corners of the children's and the flock's eyes had disappeared, as though swept by the wind to some other, less paltry place. There was never a bit of refuse in or around their camp. Any site abandoned by them in their wanderings was left as clean as on the day of Creation, there being not the smallest item, no snip of thread or broken shard, that they did not find a use for. Their lives were as lean as their bodies. Nor did it occur to them to send the Dedanites to any of the other camps. They would only find the same desolation there.

The Dedanites sent a slave to spy the Hebrews out. The man, a most ugly-looking fellow with a low brow and a split upper lip, sought out their company at once. Smiling hideously he told them that he himself was of the seed of Abraham, Isaac, and Jacob, a Hebrew whose distant ancestors had not descended to Egypt. They regarded him suspiciously, with revulsion. They could not abide his friendliness or his smiles, which were all moist red gums amid the hairs of his beard. He followed them around like a sedulous fly, picking up crying babies, helping the women to bear loads, lending a hand with the milking, tying bundles of date pomace for the flocks, and—worst of all—speaking in their own language. He showed some of the men that he was circumcised just like them. Proudly he told them how at night, when the other slaves all knelt to pray to their heathenish idols, he alone remained upright, speaking to God. Just like their forefathers beyond the River Jordan. Like Abraham, Isaac, and Jacob.

They did not know what to make of him.

And then one day, when he had stepped outside the camp to evacuate himself, Joshua's brother Yakhin approached him from behind and, as the kneeling slave turned his ugly, smiling, perpetually fawning face, coolly stabbed him once, then again, in the throat with his dagger and departed. Eshkhar witnessed it all from behind a spreading thorn tree. He shivered a bit, as if with fever, but did not give himself away. He never doubted that Yakhin had every right. He just felt a bit disappointed. Could the deed be as easy as that?

When they found their slave's body, the Dedanites raised a great hue and cry. To replace him, the best slave they ever had, they demanded three young boys from the Hebrews. And the latter had better stop pretending that they were freemen and freemen's sons. Why, the whole world knew that they were simply rebel slaves who had run away from their rightful masters in Egypt, the least of all of Pharaoh's bondsmen, a riffraff that did not even have its own god to

45

bow down to: three slaves for the murdered man and not a whit less.

Yet even as they railed and ranted, the Dedanites knew well enough that they would not get so much as a single boy. The men ringing them closely around may have looked sheepish, sullen, and not especially courageous, but their ranks were drawn tight. Soon enough indeed a screaming Dedanite who had been tearing at his beard while rolling on the ground declared that so excellent a slave as his was worth more than a hundredweight of good copper, half-a-hundredweight of gold, and twelve flasks of honey, or at least no less—and everyone sighed with relief.

There was no bargaining. The Dedanites stalked haughtily into some tents and seized what they could, crying murder all the while. With a special glee they fell upon the house of Tsuri's musical instruments, making off with them as though they had chanced on a treasure hoard. Hardly one was left unpillaged. A pallid lassitude, perhaps the inscrutable taste of guilt, hung over the camp. The incident of the Hebrew slave oppressed them all. The lady Ashlil's maid-servants hurriedly hid all her gold beneath a carpet on

46

which she lay down, but the Dedanites did not enter her tent.

Quickly they gathered the little they had found and mounted their kneeling camels, which sprang at once to their feet with their riders. Leaving the camp as swiftly as they had entered it slowly, they threatened to inform on it to the first Egyptian garrison they met, which, they said, was less than a day's march away.

The fact of the matter was that the Hebrews could have trailed them easily and taken everything back. But they were too low-spirited. A bad taste, a taste of wrongdoing and defeat, was in their mouths. The last echoing shouts died away. They were alone again, strung out in their ragged camp, in the open plain between the tamarisk and the zizyph tree, as poor as they had been before.

And yet, thought many of the camp dwellers without saying it, and yet we should have had a god to show them. So as not to be shamed.

Following this they hurriedly left the plain and walked for several days to a country of high cliffs. They marched quickly until, one evening, they made camp opposite a large outcrop of rock. They were off the caravan route and no longer needed to fear pursuit by Pharaoh, but they had left the springs behind too and arrived very thirsty. Here and there they found water in a catchment or in a trickle on a rockface that was here today and gone in tomorrow's sun. They licked the stones, panting like thirsty dogs. They did not pitch their tents that night but slept wherever they collapsed.

In the morning they rose astounded. They had heard of the mountains of the gods, but these mountains were themselves gods, the shapes and massive forms of a world that could not even have been dreamed of in flat Egypt: little wonder that the gods sometimes spoke from them, whether from a lone bramble or from a mountain itself. Forgetting their thirst, they tilted their heads and gazed upward. Some of the mountains seemed to have been created twice-over: once as the usual dirt hills or soft hummocks dotted with desert shrubs, and then, upon these, steep, perpendicular, tremendous reddish-gray walls like the wrinkled parts of a colossal, nonexistent elephant. At times these precipices made one think of a huge, abandoned workshop whose sculptor had cast down the debris from his work, which crashed down in fractured blocks and heaps of smashed little flints, all piled together in a titanic disorder. The few thorn trees at their foot looked tiny, no bigger than a man's hand. Suddenly there was a great deal of mountain and hardly any sky; yet the sky between cliff and cliff was the bluest ever seen by them, the essence, the quintessence, of sky. The light too was very strong, a clear, rocky, no longer sandy light. They felt sure that the god of these mountains must be asleep for hundreds of years. Sometimes a huge, stony, wrinkled, half-shut eye could be seen in the rockface; sometimes, it was sworn by some, its lid opened to look at those below. Had only they dared, they most certainly would have offered some sacrifice to these god-peaks, some propitiation for having infringed on their domain. But they were afraid. Here and there, in the days that followed, men and women emerging from their tents would first bow quickly, surreptitiously, to the mountain. They knew, of course, that it was not the God of the Hebrews, but who could be sure? Every little rockfall funneling down its slopes was frightening.

But the mountains remained passive. Little by little the wanderers grew accustomed to both their size and their silence. No longer did they think them sleeping gods; more likely they were great dead ones. Perhaps it was the God of their ancestors who had killed them. The black goats climbed the cliffs blithely, surefootedly, with the children on their heels. Soon their loud shouts echoed from crag to crag.

51

All these voices and all this life, though, did not penetrate very far up. There were mountains whose summits were impossible to scale, so high that even the largest birds of prey flew beneath and not above them. The Hebrews were certain that up there, in the highest places, still lived gods who could not be reached. There, way, way up, not a shrub or even a lichen could be seen, and the silence was unbroken by a single bird's call. Sometimes a cloud covered the mountaintop; then the valley beneath it was darkened by shadow and its dwellers paused mutely for an instant or two. Throughout their stay in the high mountains they felt like suffered transients, sojourners who did not really belong. The place belonged to no man, it was the demesne of its own strange gods alone. The horizontal face of Egypt, supine in the sun, was very far away.

Though the high mountains trapped a rain cloud now and then, and there were still some sparse traces of old floods in the canyons, the people were thirsty. Light reigned supreme; the heavens were open doors, open windows of it, eclipsing all lines and contours. They no longer seemed to be living in time but in light alone.

Eshkhar camped by a canyon that still had some water in

it, though this had grown brackish and was scummed over by a noxious, darkly iridescent slime. Thirst gripped them all. Each coped as best he could. They no longer boiled their food or even tried roasting it, apart from some rare, wispy little fires of twigs or broom roots that smoked discouragingly and came to nothing. Pale infants clung to their mothers' breasts, barely stirring. The flocks stood still, each ewe's head tucked under the next ewe's belly. At night the thirsty people licked dew from the rocks with their animals; by day they sucked on saltwort and its sharp, unfamiliar flavor filled their mouths. Among themselves they grumbled about this strange place, a place fit for gods but not for men. Their eyes had their fill of fine sights, yet their gullets were parched. In the end they would die amid this feral indifference and their bones would pile up in great heaps. Only the birds of prey would remain. They were waiting already. One afternoon a great sun eagle flew over the camp, gliding slowly, and with a sharp cry let fall a dead woman's arm from its beak. They were struck with dread.

The two women approached Eshkhar in his place far from camp. They walked meekly, downtroddenly, and asked with utter abjectness if he knew of any small catch-

ments that might still have some rainwater in them. They
knew, they said, that their family, the house of Tsuri, was
far from the foremost of Israel's tribes, yet their infants
were sick. Here, he could see for himself the children they
were carrying; their breasts were dry and there was no
water. Eshkhar looked at them as if impaled on a stake. Only
now did he see how the desert had ravaged the house of
Tsuri, which had languished more and more since the sack
of its instruments. The two women looked barely alive.
Why had they come to him, he asked. Why had they not
gone to Moses? Let him work them a miracle. He, Eshkhar, was not a miracle man. Did they think that he was
Moses that they expected him to restore the milk to their
dugs? There were, replied the women, more important people than themselves who had business with Moses; great
crowds besieged his tent every day, clamoring for water.
They regarded him as they spoke with their large, beaten
eyes that were sloe-shaped like those of the whole house of
Tsuri's. Each of them hesitantly fingered the skirt of her
dress, rolling it back and forth with her free hand. They
knew that a man could do only so much.

He said that he would try. That he would look. That he

54

could not be sure. He searched for a long while, scaling
with difficulty the high, craggy cliffs, following the calls of
the birds. Once or twice a clump of greenery misled him.
Finally, after much time had elapsed, he found a puddle that
still had not dried out completely. Removing his headcloth,
he soaked up all its water and ran back down to the women.
They were waiting patiently just where he had left them.
Not a word seemed to have passed between them in his ab-
sence. The arms of their infants, hot and insentient, dangled down. He handed them the sopping cloth, for which
they thanked him submissively; then, tearing it carefully in
two, they stuck each half in the mouth of a child and headed
back to camp.

The next day the people were told that Moses would
bring them water.

They stood, as though in a narrow alleyway, in a white,
very deep canyon. One could tell by the birds, which flew
low between the canyon walls chattering in loud voices,
that there once had been water here. The shrubbery too
bore witness to an underground source. Now, however,
there was nothing, only a very slow trickle from a single
crevice, one drop at a time that took forever to gather and

swell until, bursting at last, it cast itself off from the whitish rock and plunged downward. Followed, after a long interval, by another. The walls of the canyon were steep and its floor was littered with flattened white rocks like petrified bedding. There was a smell of dry mold in the air. They stood jammed together at the canyon's bottom end, surrounded by echoes, overhung by a great deal of rock.

Eshkhar stood at the canyon's top end, watching detachedly. The crowd of people was very large. Among the flat rocks were still a few puddles of scummy green water in which the great throng sloshed its feet. Some held empty flasks or water jugs. Soon there would be water. Moses had said so.

The two women whose babies were dying of thirst stood off to one side too. Though the rags from Eshkhar's headcloth were still in the infants' mouths, they no longer had the strength to suck. Most likely the cloth was dry anyway. Red-faced and lifeless, a dark slit of eye stewing beneath each heavy lid like black, boiling mud, they let their little arms hang limply. Their hands already looked dead.

And then, all at once, Moses' party arrived walking

quickly. The crowd jostled to make way for it, a highly com-
pact group clad conspicuously in white, squeezed almost
shoulder to shoulder with Moses in its midst. His tall staff
issued above it like the mast of a white boat that cleft a swift
course among the throng.

The group reached the front rock and broke ranks, so
that Moses could take his place at its head. It was Eshkhar's
one fleeting glimpse of him, a man with probing eyes and
a pugnaciously outthrust beard, yet now grim and remote.
He seemed impatient, as if eager to get on unhindered with
the job. From the rear, as though he were their prisoner, his
white-clad escort closed in on him again.

For a moment, like a craftsman gauging his work, he appeared to measure the thickness and height of the rock;
then, without warning, lifting his staff straight in front of
him like a crowbar, he jabbed the bottom of it down on the
white slab between his feet; with which, not even waiting
to see what would happen, the white group spun around as
one man and started back. The crowd, however, paid it no
attention, for all eyes were on the chalky rock. There could
be no doubt of it: the slow trickle increased from one mo-

ment to the next, the drops at first growing larger and more frequent, then joining to form a threadlike jet that turned almost at once into a real spout of water.

Jubilantly, exultantly, they ran yelling to fill their flasks and jugs. A frightful brawl broke out by the rock. The canyon was very narrow, and in the strife, people were crushed against its walls. Others pushed, shoved, cursed, struck, and stepped on each other. Unnoticed, two men were trampled to death near the outflow. Yet the water kept on gushing as though it had never done anything else.

In all this commotion the two women were unable to reach it. Duress had overcome them and left them too weak to fight. In any case, their babies were no longer alive. Moses and his escort passed by without seeing them. Hopelessly, they stood staring at the wall of flowing water and at the hideous, fatal fracas taking place there. The infants' arms dangled earthward, obviously dead.

That night heavy clouds hid the stars. A cold, very strong wind began to blow. Toward morning a downpour fell and filled all the catchments and water holes. The canyon was flooded. The birds returned to it at sunup, chattering loudly in low flight. The sated bushes and maidenhead ferns glistened wetly.

They buried the dead. The two mothers buried their babies too and returned, without a word, to their daily chores. They had nothing more to say, neither to Moses nor to Eshkhar. They avoided him, as thin and bent as before.

A year or two after this Baita went looking for Eshkhar. Her
two children had a stomach ailment and she professed to be
going to gather caltrop bark for a remedy. In truth, however, she headed for the furthest flocks.

Eshkhar noticed her almost at once. As usual he was pas-
turing his flock far from camp, and the form of the woman
that suddenly entered his vision, looming enormous on a
nearby hill, shook him to the quick. Although she saw him
too, she gave no sign of it. She stood opposite him for a
while, then went on foraging on the hillside. Eshkhar

stared hard at her without moving, flooded by wave after wave of savage emotion.

Then Baita descended the hill and his heart stopped its terrible pounding.

The next day, and the day after that, she came back. Each time, enormous, alone in the world, she appeared on the same hillside, foraged for a while, gazed at him, and disappeared. His nights were sleepless. Bundled in the warm breath and warm wool of his bleating flock, he lay wide awake looking up at the sky of big stars.

After that Baita came no more.

And one day he entered camp on the run, his eyes shut like those of a man plunging into deep water. Mingling with the crowd he made his way past the tents, past the camp of Levi, past the camp of Reuben, pressing swiftly ahead to the camp of Ephraim, his heart ready to burst. He was sure that he would find her. His legs carried him by themselves.

Baita was sitting in her tent, nursing her youngest child; yet without heeding its protests she put it down the moment he burst inside. Panting, he stood facing her. She went to the water jug, from whose neck hung a cup, and poured him a drink that he downed in one gulp, without stopping for breath, holding the cup out for more. She refilled it. This time he drank more slowly, watching her over the rim, his grave eyes dark and deep. He seemed to be all eyes; all-seeing; and he held her eyes with his own as though binding them to him. Her eyelids trembled. She wanted to shut them but could not.

She herself blocked the tent opening with fardels of twigs. Whose if not his could she be?

Afterwards she cried from emotion and a bit from fear too. Eshkhar's temples were alabaster white. He pressed her close and wiped away her tears, promising to take her far, far away. She nodded, not knowing whether she was happy or miserable. Things had become too much for her. Yet even as he spoke Eshkhar knew well enough that there was no place for him to take her and no place for them to go. Beyond the pillar of smoke there was nothing.

Baita was afraid. So deathly afraid that she almost panicked. During their infrequent meetings she took to pushing Eshkhar away from her, her hands shaking, her pupils contracted. Her father and mother would kill her. They would publicly stone her. Zavdi would murder the children. He held her palsied body, weeping with fear, in his arms. Once he even struck her. In the end she confessed that she was afraid of Moses, only of him. He had ways of finding out everything in the world, on earth, in heaven, even in the stones. That was what made her limbs shrink. Perhaps she had been ill all along, or perhaps her illness was caused by her fear. She was a strong woman and fought it for as long as she could. Yet eventually she took to her bed, rivulets of sweat pouring off her, her hands clawing the rug, her feet twitching, until, midway through a spasm, she turned as hard as a rock and was at peace. Zavdi, crying hotly and copiously, brought her to her grave.

Eshkhar went back to his mountain.

He did so because he wanted nothing to do with God. Others had their escapes; for him there was none. His stay in the camp had flayed him alive. Each sickness, each misery, every pain, was suffered in his own flesh. If a child was beaten, the beating was given to him; if a man cried at night, the tears were his own. He roamed the camp, an echo of everyone's hurt, until he nearly collapsed. The agony of Baita had become for him the agony of the whole world, and he had no protection against it. He felt that he was going mad in this place. From afar there would be no need to see them all, to think of them all, of every diseased, or blinded, or dying man, of everyone who was oppressed. The fate of Baita and the fate of his mother, Milka, merged for him into one indistinguishable whole. His life in camp had become a horror. Among its dwellers he was vulnerable and exposed, incapable of forgetting, powerless to heal.

At heart he knew that he could not wander far beyond the pillars of smoke and fire, but still he tried. He began to explore the desert a day or two's walk at a time. He found valleys paved with huge slabs of stone like highways; he found canyons in which grew hawthorn and quince trees; he found graves, and temples, and queer manmade structures, and bones. During one of these excursions to nowhere he fell and broke his ankle. Somehow he hobbled back, but the bone knitted badly and left him with a limp. He grew used to knotting a thick rope around it and walking with the aid of it.

Having no friends, he had habits. Every day had its set routine. He no longer desired visitors, who would only get in the way. He stayed or went exploring as he pleased. He found no other gods in the desert. But he did find other destinies.

Once, having climbed to the top of a mountain, he was made to gasp for breath: across the valley beneath him, clearly belonging to someone, set amid a covey of fruiting trees that grew closely around it, stood a house. He waited for darkness to come, then slipped quietly down to it and pressed himself against a crack in a wall. In the large room sat a couple, a man and a woman, their disproportionately short legs folded under them, their rigid faces staring straight ahead. Their chairs were made of a rich, dark wood covered with strange drawings and engravings. In the woman's lap, its eyes shut, lay a cat.

Eshkhar was appalled beyond words. Why then, he thought dimly, all their wandering in the desert, all their misery, all the death from thirst and disease? Hobbling on his bad foot he fled for dear life, running night and day until he rejoined his flock, his ears ringing from the pace and from the insoluble riddle that left him utterly blank. In the end he realized that he would never solve it. He was no longer even sure that he had seen what he thought he had, or that, should he ever go back, he would see it again. The wild notion that things might be otherwise faded and died away. Once more the desert closed in on him. He grew deeper into himself.

Not once did he dream of Baita. It was as if she had journeyed far away from him, so far that there was no telling where.

So that, returning one day with some newborn kids in his arms, he was startled to find, their hair grown wild, Aviel, Yakhin, and Zemer sitting and waiting awkwardly for him outside his tent. They embraced, then jostled each other a bit as they had done when they were children, until each came to rest on one foot, from which they vehemently continued their bumping, hopping about like chickens and laughing helplessly. Aviel was the first to collapse on the ground, followed by Zemer; soon after which all four of them lay in one heap, wiping their eyes. Then they rose and trooped into the small tent. Eshkhar was embarrassed to have nothing to serve them. If only they would wait a bit, he would go fetch a kid, milk a goat. But they had not come for that, they said; they had come for a word with him. In the tattered tent with its habitual reek of dried-dung fuel,

goat hair and broken wind they told him that he was
smarter than any of them, that he had known, cunning
rogue that he was, just when to leave the camp. Now every
man jack of them was set to leave too. Moses had gone off
somewhere, no one knew for how long, while Joshua sat at
the entrance to his tent lording it over them all. For some
time the people had been saying that they had had enough
of wandering about the desert at Moses' beck and call, one
day to the lowlands and the next to the highlands, now to
die of illness and now of thirst, never knowing the where
or the why of it. They were turning into a shameless mob,
like the first castaways who had left Egypt long before them.
They were all castaways now.

—We came forth from Egypt, said Aviel in his soft voice,
we came forth from Egypt, Eshkhar, we left the house of
bondage, and now we are pining away in this desert and are
going to die in it. Why, even if Moses wanted the whole
generation that left Egypt to be killed off here, it's the children who are dying in our arms, not the old men. We've dug
more graves than we can count, and there's still no end in
sight.

And Zemer added:

68

—We must honor our children that their days be long upon this earth. The people are stealing from each other's tents, Eshkhar, it's like a plague of locusts in the camp. Men have even been murdered because of it. But we shall not steal nor murder. And none of us shall rule another or tell him when to work and when to rest. Because that's why we left the house of bondage, so as not to be slaves anymore. And there shall be no lies among us. Only if each man loves his neighbor will there be peace in our camp.

Eshkhar asked what they would do if the people did not let them go. We shall have to wait and see what we do then, said Aviel uncertainly. Though Yakhin says that we will smite them.

Eshkhar glanced at Yakhin. He sat muscular and taciturn, playing with his short dagger and gazing tranquilly back as if to confirm the execution of the harelipped Dedanite slave. If the people do not let us go, said his perfectly still eyes to Eshkhar, then they are a people of slaves and will be cut down just as he was. Did you not see for yourself how easy it was to kill?

Aviel, though, sought to temper things, to be vague, to say nothing so outright that it left no room for retreat.

69

There were so few of them, he said. Most of the people were so much grass to be trampled on. They rose like dumb animals, and went to bed like dumb animals, and were led about from mountain to mountain like dumb animals by Moses, on and on and on. That was why the three of them had come to Eshkhar. They wanted to ask him to come down to the camp with them at once, before Moses returned, since as soon as he did the people would follow him again like mooncalves, even right into their graves. Now is the time, they said. And headed back.

Warily, cautiously, gradually, Eshkhar moved his flock back toward the camp, advancing a little each day. Already he could clearly see and hear the hubbub of life at the foot of the high mountain. The winter was over. The canyons were full of water and the valley had sprouted everywhere with patches of green. Countless flowers covered the hillsides: bean caper, and stinkweed, and yellow primroses, and the fierce purple of the henbane. The people had risen from their former dejection; the curtain of despondency that had accompanied them from Egypt seemed to have lifted. The valley hummed as if each pair of hands were busy looking for something to do, as if many thoughts, songs, woonings, were circulating through it. That winter, for the first time in their lives, they had seen and been terrified by the snow in the high mountains. Most of the graves on the bottom slopes were of children and infants who had died from the cold. The night frosts had gnawed at them mercilessly. Now the sun warmed their bones and straightened their spines, and with it came a surge of new strength.

Eshkhar felt restored too. The people he met when he finally came into camp were happy to see him, as he was to see them. He ate real, honestly ground and baked bread. Disheveled, chastened, he sat with his friends thinking what a fine fool he had been. Why, he was flesh of their flesh.

They were not alone in their discontent. Elsewhere, in other tents, groups of men had formed too, some of whom were even thinking of breaking away and returning to Egypt. Of kneeling before Pharaoh and begging forgiveness. Anything was better than this pointless wandering. The camp was full of rebellion. Only the castaways, as usual, laughed unbelievingly. It won't get you anywhere, they said. You had better get used to it right now. Moses will cook you all for breakfast when he gets back and still have room left for dessert. When asked with whom they would go should one of the tribes head off on its own, they replied: with Moses and the Levites, of course, they have the sharpest knives. They laughed and laughed. Their laughter grew to be unbearable.

Now Yonat, sister of Aviel, a twitch-faced woman, squatted with them also by the entrance to Aviel's tent. Sometimes she puckered her brow, giving her a sourish look; other times she opened her mouth wide or tilted her head to one side while nodding up and down as though chewing; always, though, her eyes were big, and worlds came and went in them as she listened to the men talk. She herself, born mute, had never been heard to utter a word; yet they always knew what she felt, for her emotions seemed to emanate through her black dress with a fiercely domineering smell. She had in her the power of all pent-up things. Though they ignored her presence, they were strongly aware of it. She always sat on the ground by the tent flap, very quiet and intense.

All at once Yonat leaped from her squat and tore the earrings from her ears, the right lobe's with her right hand and the left lobe's with her left, both in a single motion. Very quickly now, her ears bleeding, she ran from man to man, from woman to woman, her feet skimming into tents and down paths, her gory earrings held out in one hand, mutely demanding, mutely seizing their gold, hurdling tent pegs and tent stays, impatient of ties and clasps, into tents, down paths, her hand extended, making dark sounds in her throat. As a man running with a lit torch sets all around him on fire, so did Aviel's twitch-faced sister Yonat run quickly, setting the camp on fire with a dark, unholy flame. No one dared resist her. No one had the strength to match hers. Perhaps the spirit of the god of the moutains had entered into her. A few women ran to hide from her; yet by now she was trailed by a retinue of men who themselves stripped the indignantly screaming holdouts of their adornments. The gold was brought to the center court of the tribe, where, like some precious scrap metal, it lay on a sheepskin in a jagged, angular pile, gleaming with its own amassed insolence.

They gathered round the sheepskin. The pile was small, barely a few fistfuls of gold. They stood staring at it, as if forced to realize just how paltry their wealth was, just how puny their strength, when the lady Ashlil, her face old and naked without its jewelry, suddenly appeared with a large

straw basket and emptied it over the pile. They were over-
joyed to see that her gold covered all of theirs.

Stark against the rocks in her black dress, her gory ears
a red trickle, Yonat ran quickly through the valley to the
tents of the neighboring tribes. There too a great uproar
broke out. The day was still young and the sun still high
overhead when several men flushed with excitement came
to take the gold to the main pile by the great fire at the front
end of the camp.

Things had got out of hand. The day's chores forgotten,
they stood uncertainly in the openings of their tents listening to the distant stir. Some, making up their minds with
a sheepish shrug, slipped off to see for themselves the huge
blaze in which the gold was being melted down. A strong
smell, a great deal of smoke, and an uneasy sensation, as of
some planned festivity gone awry, hung over the camp. Ab-
sently the women ran their hands over their legs denuded
of anklets and bangles. All of a sudden there was an unac-
customed, a springlike, a disquieting lightness in the air.
Without a god, without a leader, they inhaled smoke and
waited.

Eshkhar heard the tumult from afar and limped hur-

riedly into camp on his lame leg, wondering. At the canyon's end he met Aviel, who, flushed and good-humored,
hugged him mollifyingly around the shoulders: there's no
harm in it, Eshkhar, no harm. Let the people have their day.
Tomorrow we shall be the wiser.

The blood rushed to Eshkhar's head. Overflowing with
anger he strove to slip free of Aviel's grasp, which only,
however, grew stronger: no harm in it, Eshkhar, no harm,
a spirit got into Yonat. No one could stop her, she swept
everyone with her. And up there, by the column of smoke,
there was a miracle, a real miracle, Eshkhar. When all that
gold was melted down, it came out looking like an ox.
Maybe it's Chemosh. No one touched that gold with his
hand, Eshkhar, and still it turned into an ox. It has to be a
miracle. You can't fight miracles, Eshkhar!

Panting like two evenly matched wrestlers in the stream-
bed, they stood for a long moment in a frozen embrace,
muscles strained, necks crimson, brows bulging, until Eshkhar fought loose of Aviel's stranglehold, threw him vio-
lently to the ground, and ran back, containing his limp until
he was over the hill. Aviel picked himself up and ran quickly
to the fire, where he was swallowed up by the crowd.

Thick smoke and loud cries spread out over the desert, above which wafted a smell of great unease. Eshkhar ran back to his tent and lay down there, burying his sweaty face in his sheepskin. He knew now that his life would be lived out without them, just as theirs would be lived out without him. This was the first and would be the last time that he had betrayed his own solitude. They had sought to seduce him with their freshly baked bread and the treacherous swamp of their friendship, and he had almost let them succeed.

He groaned and gnashed his teeth, squirming where he lay. Back there a few flutes were wailing and men and women, the last survivors of the house of Tsuri, were singing; all evening long, far into the night, sheep were slaughtered to the muffled beat of drums and the billows of reveling smoke. Nowhere in the whole desert was there any escape. A band of raucous youths passed near his tent, howling as they ran. Later a couple that had slipped away from camp came to look for a trysting place and found one not far from him; tormented by their moans and whispers, he could not stop his ears. Tossing on the ground, whimpering to himself like a dog, he lay totally alone in the world.

But there too the revelry turned to groans. The sky had yet to pale when fierce brawls broke out, at the center of which were the bedaggered sons of Levi. Before dawn broke, large groups of unarmed men began fleeing to their tents with cries of horror, leaving hundreds of mutilated bodies behind them. It was later said that Joshua himself ran his brother Yakhin through. A pallid sun rose to shine on the many corpses, on the gnawed cattle bones by the fire, on the overturned pots, and on the wilted flowers drooping from the golden idol that no longer looked like anything at all. It was difficult to fathom how anyone could have thought it an ox or a calf. A cracked silence reigned. Dragging bowed legs, her clothes in tatters, her mouth askew, Yonat was the last to stagger back to the tents at the rear of the camp.

Moses returned to find a gray, extinguished camp that had shut itself up in its tents and did not care to remember what had happened.

They buried their dead and submitted to the Law.

From that day on Moses too seemed a cleft man. At last he told them that they were going to the Ancestral Land. Sadly he spoke to them of blessings, of curses—all, all of which they accepted as though it were their daily bread and they, his day laborers, were hangdoggedly taking it from his hands. They could hardly look each other in the eye. He talked on about olives, about grapes, about pomegranates, about figs, and wearily they answered yes, yes, anything you say, as long as we don't all have to drop dead in this desert, amen. No, they would make no more statues or graven images. Yes, they would not murder. They would not bear false witness. Whatever he told them, amen.

But Eshkhar knew none of all this. He had struck out so far on his own that the pillars of smoke and of fire were no longer in sight, nor did he wish them to be. The camp could go its way and he would go his. He had no notion of where it was headed for, if it was headed anywhere at all.

For many years, perhaps ten, perhaps more, he wandered by himself in the desert, alone with his flock. If the others crossed it once, he did so dozens of times. And he knew things that they did not: that the desert was inhabited, that it had limits, that it could be crossed from end to end in a matter of weeks. The deception of miracles was keeping them purblind and lost.

Often he took his flock grazing to the north, near the caravan route. Once he saw a party of Dedanites. Though he thought they were the same traders who had plundered them soon after they left Egypt, he could not be sure. There came back to him the memory of the harelipped slave, and with it a heavy, obscure grief. He would have given a great deal to be able to bring that man with his ugly red lip, his fawning smiles, and his dextrous hands back to life. A man should die for his own sins alone, he told himself, knowing that that would never be. Not even with God. It was too easy to kill, to knife, to send disease.

Now and then he saw detachments of Pharaoh's troops clattering loudly toward one of the forts that lined the way. He never hid from them, yet they paid him no heed. Once a caravan passed quickly by bearing the murderer of his mother, the Canaanite overseer, now great and wealthy, who was on his way back to Canaan. But Eshkhar did not know this. He saw only a rich man—some lord, no doubt— with his face concealed from the burning sun, and many slaves. They galloped by, kicking up great clouds of dust. Had they stopped to ask him for water, he would surely have drawn it for them from the well.

From God there came no accounting, neither by day nor by night, when the huge stars hung in their orbits overhead. Sometimes he thought that he was god himself. Once he traveled far to the east and knew without being told that he was in the Ancestral Land. He asked for the name of an oasis and was answered Beersheba, the Well of the Oath. When he went southward from there, descending more and more until he felt sure that he had reached the bottom of the

81

world, he found a slate-colored sea whose odd waters smelled of sulfur. Marveling greatly, he returned. And yet that too was not the world's end.

None of this was known in the camp. They wandered on. No one asked anymore why they lingered so long in the desert. No one knew why they camped in one place for two weeks and in another for two or five years. If no rains fell, they sowed in dry ground and pounded the meager yield into a coarse flour. It was hard to imagine that there once had been a world apart from this desert, their only home, their only love, their birthplace and burial ground. Most of those who had left Egypt were no longer alive. The others, like doorless and windowless houses, had no other memories. Life in the desert consumed them utterly and left nothing over. Was there really any place else? One might see a bronzed youth grab a ewe, grip her tightly by her thin legs, sprawl out with her on his chest, and drink straight from her udders. Who needed a bowl? The women scolded them, but they just laughed and kept on. Theirs was a carefree generation. Instead of memories they had the new law. It never occurred to them to challenge it. If asked, they would have answered: it is a good law.

Once they came to a shore with a very flat sea, and a salt
marsh, and open spaces, and feathery rushes, and a beati-
tude of date palms, and soft, soft surf that spilled onto the
sand with warm whispers, a balm for body and soul. In the
shallow water stood a jungle of mangrove trees, their roots
thick and exposed like the ropes of a fisherman's nets. A
kingfisher stood with its head in the water, unafraid. It felt
good to be out of the rocky clefts and canyons and to stretch
out peacefully with no other sound than the softly sighing
surf, or sometimes the splash of a springing fish as it broke
water, or the thin, barely audible scrape of the translucent
little crabs tracing a line in the foam. The camp eased itself
down in great silence, breathing in and out with the breath
of the sea, filling its lungs, its whole self with it, letting
the blessedness course slowly through it with each hushed
pause between wave and wave.

For two or three weeks they immersed themselves in the
murmur of the sea, the soughing of the date palms, and the
abundance of fish; then they gathered their possessions
and headed back into the maw of the desert. All of them,
that is, except for a few remaining families of the castaways,
who told Moses that they were staying right here, on this

shore. They were not meant, they explained apologetically, for so much governance and laws. His "Thou shalt not steal" was too much for them. They had better stay where they were and not spoil the order of things.

The others pushed on. Long afterwards they remembered that shore with longing, until it too ceased to be a shore in space and became one in time, which they would always seek to return to and would never be able to find. Another year passed and it was no longer even mentioned.

And then one day Eshkhar, slowly climbing a hill, saw the pillar of smoke in front of him.

Gingerly he edged nearer, careful to pitch his tent at a safe distance. He had not seen them for years and could not now prevail upon himself to flee at once. He would, he decided, observe them for a few more days, another week, then move on before he was noticed. Yet more time went by and he remained, staring thoughtfully at the pillar of smoke by day and at the pillar of fire by night, telling himself every day that tomorrow he would be gone. The next day, though, he was still there.

Once, returning to his tent, he noticed a new smell. He looked about and, to his surprise, saw that someone had cleaned his rugs and cooking pots and wet down the floor of the tent. The strange smell gave him no peace.

The same thing happened the next day and the day after that; each day the strange smell of camphorwood clashed with his own stench and the reek of the broom-root coals until the new smell vanquished the old. On the fourth day he spied the woman slipping away from his tent. He overtook her easily and dragged her back with him. She looked at him without fear. As he made her yield he saw that she had six fingers on each hand. She was not a virgin.

She told him that her name was Dina and that, like him, she lived outside the camp and not in her father's tents; indeed, she did not even know who her father was. Slowly, gently, she undid the rough rope that had bound his ankle for years and massaged the bone; then she brought wet leaves and tied them in its place. He himself had made such poultices for his flock and, grumbling a bit, submitted to her fingers. Yet he did not permit her to spend the night in his tent. At sundown she rose without a word and went back to where she had come from.

That night, for the first and last time, he dreamed of Baita. She stood smiling at him as if all were forgiven, as if to let him know that everything was all right. Then, leaning toward him to kiss him farewell with an utter, peaceful finality, she vanished. He woke crying hard.

Dina came back. A few days later she told him in her low voice why she lived outside the camp. She had, she said, conceived out of wedlock and was afraid to go back; if he would testify that she was his wedded wife, she might live; otherwise she was as good as dead already. She spoke perfectly calmly, as calmly as she folded her strange hands that had six fingers on them. When he replied gruffly that she could tell them whatever she wished, she kissed his hands with joy. Sometimes she bent over him and wrapped him in her long hair as though it were a tent.

Once he asked about her fingers. She said she was born that way, to a father whom she did not know, which was why she was considered impure; it was an act of mercy, she had been told, that she was not killed at birth, though she herself sometimes wondered about this; for because of it she had been given to no one in marriage, albeit a certain man from her tribe, a kinsman of hers, or at least so he claimed, had lain with her from time to time until he had got her with child. Observing her, Eshkhar noticed for the first time that her deep-set eyes had the beaten look of the house of Tsuri's eyes in the desert. Perhaps she was all that remained of it. No one had taught her to play music, though. Nor would there have been anything to play it on.

Another time he asked her about his friends Aviel, Yakhin, and Zemer. She told him what she knew: that Zemer was alive and well and the father of many children, and that Aviel had died in battle. He had not even known that there had been a battle, and said nothing for a long while.

When her belly began to swell, she went away. He did not go down into the camp to look for her.

Once more they were on the move. A party of scouts returned with some grape leaves and raisins. They told of huge grapevines that bore wondrous fruit, and of others, fed by a great spring, that scaled high walls. Slowly they began to believe that there was an end to their trek. That the Ancestral Land existed. Once some young men brought back a few olive branches that moved the lady Ashlil to tears. Taking them, she pressed them to her heart. At last, at long last, she said, she had seen the branch of the olive tree; never had she thought that she would live to see the day. All her life she had wanted to see one just once. Jugs of olive oil she had seen, but never a real branch. Now she could die content.

Dina returned with a child in her arms. Watching her sit quietly nursing it, Eshkhar felt a deep peace. He knew that with peace, compassion would come back too, but he no longer had the strength to fight it. One day Dina threw away the rope with which he kept retying his ankle. You don't need it anymore, Eshkhar, she said. He tried taking a step or two and saw that she was right. When winter came with its cold and fierce winds, she took to sleeping in his tent with her son, nor did he turn her out anymore. Once he asked her tauntingly, what about the miracles, were there still many miracles in camp—to which, after mulling it over, she answered that, although she was not sure, it seemed to her that, at least as far as she remembered, the miracles had stopped long ago. They simply had kept plodding on.

Then she conceived Eshkhar's child and, when her time came, went down to the midwives in camp and gave birth to Yotam. And an auspicious birth it was.

Toward the end time itself seemed to go mad and the
days and nights chased each other faster and faster. They
marched quickly and covered distances greater than any
they had covered before. The terrain was rolling now, almost open, and the Land was nearer every day. They no
longer had the patience for the routines of desert life, and
seldom even pitched their tents when they camped at night.
More often they simply curled up in their woolen sheep-
skins and slept under the sky. The women stopped weaving,
the old men gave up making baskets. Their belongings were

rarely unpacked. Were it not for the elders, who counted each day and religiously kept track of the holy days, they would have lost all sense of time. In the sky, upon the rocks, in the thickets of thorn trees, they could now make out the birds of a cultivated land.

Gradually, almost imperceptibly, the pillar of flame had been dimming. It burned less brightly and, like a candle in the dawn, had lost its luster. Glancing at its smoldering edges, they felt no grief. They knew that the Land was close by now; those who had pushed ahead of the camp had even glimpsed it beyond a rift-valley whose bottom was too deep to be seen, a long range of mountains that ran the whole length of the horizon, covered by a gray haze. As they approached the haze turned purplish brown, sometimes almost gold, as though bathed in heavenly grace.

More and more people were pressing ahead to see now, as if they were standing on the deck of a ship nearing land, which loomed larger the closer they came. And yet it was hard to say if they were progressing toward it or if it was coming to meet them, so massive, so majestically colored, though its details were still undivulged.

Not only had the pillar of flame begun to fade, Moses

too was no longer the man he once was. His mind was fail-
ing. Sometimes, imagining that *ba* and *ka* had come to take
his soul, he harangued them that he was a Hebrew, not an
Egyptian, and that they should go somewhere else. Sometimes he shouted that he must, must enter the land and that
no force in heaven or on earth could stand in his way. In his
more lucid moments he sought to impose more and more
laws on them, a never-ending Torah. Yet even his intimates
no longer bothered to write them down. They knew that
his hour was nigh; one way or another, everything was already up to Joshua.

Several of the tribes were by now in the Land. No one
knew exactly how the order of entry was decided. Those
who had entered in the first or second year, it was said, had
already fought several wars. The others had to wait.

Eshkhar kept back. The Land stretched out before him
along the horizon. He stared at it as if seeking to pierce its
misty veil, to make out houses, trees, and wells, but it was
too far. He had been standing like that a long time when,
as though awakening into a dream, he sensed a strange presence behind him, unfamiliar yet perfectly clear. An indefin-
able fear kept him from turning around.

Baita? he wondered out loud. But it was not Baita. Something, someone, was calling laughingly to him from the wind, from the mountains, perhaps from the long-remembered years of wandering, someone smiling and forebearing who expected something of him without his knowing what it was. No, it is not the quail, Eshkhar, nor the manna, nor the water from the rock, called the strange presence, which was perhaps only a gentle and belated insight; it's none of these, not even Moses himself; you are close now, Eshkhar, very close; just one more little effort and you will understand.

But he could not understand. He rubbed his eyes, no longer sure that anyone, or anything, had been there. Nor, when he turned around, was there anything except the soft sandstone hills falling away to the desert. He shook his head, as if trying to rid himself of a bothersome thought; then, all at once, like a man who has not done so for years, he began to laugh.

He was heard by Yotam, who had been sent by his mother with a message. Doggedly the boy clambered up the slope, bearing down hard on his bare feet, until his father bent toward him and helped him up the last bit. Dina wanted to tell him that tomorrow the last of the camp was crossing the Jordan. She wished to know if he would come with them. And Eshkhar nodded that he would.

The boy started back down; quickly, though, Eshkhar collected himself and slid after him, taking him by the hand and returning with him to the camp. He stayed with Dina that night. The children pressed their little bodies against him. Dina snored a bit where she lay. Yet all his thoughts, and the many people packing, tying knots, and talking in the moonlight, kept him from shutting his eyes. He had told no one that he had already been in the Ancestral Land.

At last their turn came to enter.

They kept on crossing the river, household after household, family after family, men, women, and many children, those born in the desert and those who had walked all the way from Egypt. They crossed over in good order, helping each other, the good, the bad, the cruel, and the indifferent, the law-makers and the law-abiders. The flocks crossed tied to long poles, bleating with fright. A few lambs that were tied too loosely were swept away by the current. Someone lost a sandal in the river, bent to retrieve it, slipped, fell, and was stepped on by two men bunched close behind him who could not stop in time; at once, however, he was helped back to his feet. The current was strong. Some women lost their bundles, which were carried away downstream, but kept going. The ford was uneven: in places the water was shallow, while in others it rose without warning nearly waist-high. And still they crossed, a living, unswerving river of mankind bisecting the river of water. Aviel's daughter crossed, and the house of Yitzhar, and Zemer with all his large household. Two young men bore the lady Ashlil, sitting up, tightly bound to a litter, cadaverous, bald, her tiny face wrinkled and old. No one knew for sure whether she had died long ago and this was only her corpse, or whether there was still a remnant of life in her.

They kept on crossing. Those in front were already on the opposite bank, the corners of their garments knotted tightly around their waists, their brown legs gleaming with water. Like a flock of long-legged river birds they stamped hard on the sand to shake off the drops, each of them making a small puddle. Then they wrung out their clothes.

And still they kept on. Those who had crossed now stood in a broad, spacious plain whose light was white and expansive. Beyond it rose soft hills that seemed wrapped in a fine, wrinkled silk of a color sometimes white, sometimes eggshell, while set further back were slopes with green growth leading up to a towering wall that they would yet have to climb. They could sense that beyond that high ridge were more mountains, but that it was no more than a short march to the last mountain of all, to the end of all their journeys.

Far to their right stood a city, a place of many date palms splashed with the luxuriant red flowers of a tree they failed to recognize. It was all so new, fresh and sparkling. Their senses swooned before the sudden shock of oleander and flame trees, bees and turtledoves, the strong odors and the barking of the dogs. Some of them looked covetously at the inhabited city. Yet none dared reach out to pluck a single flower or fruit. The black goats alone had already plunged headlong into the bushes, which they started to devour until rounded up. There were butterflies. There were low-flying birds plummeting among the fruit trees. The people looked and looked, dumbstruck, and still they could not look enough.

Afterwards, like beads falling off a string, first two, then three, then five of them broke away from the crowd and

95

nimbly began climbing the mountain. The others followed. The flocks trotted beside them, waves of scent wash-
ing over their flared nostrils.

And when the first of them were over the ridge, no one
was left in the desert.

Design by David Bullen
Typeset in Mergenthaler Galliard
by Wilsted & Taylor
Printed by Haddon Craftsmen
on acid-free paper